# THE BLUE PERIOD

## OTHER BOOKS BY SERPENT CLUB PRESS:

**Autumn, Again; Spring, Anew**
Michael Skelton & Stephen Morel

**A Quarter Century**
Eda Gasda

**Circumambulate**
Daniel Bossert

**Moon on Water**
Matthew Gasda

**On Bicycling: An Introduction**
Samuel Atticus Steffen

**Sonata for Piano and Violin**
Matthew Gasda

**The Substitute**
Michael Skelton

**What Was Left Of The Stars**
Claire Åkebrand

**And Our Journal**
New Writing: Volume I
New Writing: Volume 2
New Writing: Volume 3

# THE BLUE PERIOD

*a novel by*
Matthew Gasda

SERPENT CLUB PRESS

The Blue Period
Copyright © Serpent Club Press, 2020
All rights reserved

For more information please contact Serpent Club Press at editor@serpentclub.org

Serpent Club Press books may be purchased for educational, business, or sales promotional use. For more information please contact Serpent Club Press at editor@serpentclub.org

First Edition

Printed in the United States of America
Set in Williams Caslon
Designed by Emily Gasda

ISBN
9780997613476

*Special thanks to Lexi for the manic, yet gentle,
editing this book needed.*

*for Melissa*

*When yawning, the human being himself opens like an abyss. He makes himself resemble the time stagnating around him.*

WALTER BENJAMIN

*Hit was gret wonder that Nature Myght suffre any creature To have such sorwe, and be not ded*

GEOFFREY CHAUCER

It's raining today because that's what the spring is for and because it's the beginning of a book

the twisted syntax of your speech seeking sight and like a downpour you painted the world with your presence and in the fragments of a dead language I named you Lost Love

Horus weeping in the desert I'll pour cool milk in your eyes muddy sunglow slides across the periphery of the earth's shadow half-asleep raise a hand stop a dream from crying out

witness-bearer born in the terrible west a wave in a vacuum distorts the speed of light seal off the eruptive shocks haul down this chain of figuration back into silence

collapsed inward like a star dislocated from its joint in space no name but wind which drags the constellations through the sky I hear myself as through another voice emptied of its extralunar music

like a ghost in a Tibetan nightmare quick moons like bright foxes night after night my dreams grow shorter

time deposited like calcium in a rock

pick the thread up anywhere follow it back
to the source of the imagination slay the
half-human beast of the heart while kings
in golden suits ride elephants over the
mountains and black stars cluster thick as
reeds in a stream

find a secret path back home I'm dreaming
of my lost interior life like a refugee from a
lost empire

rough seas to the land of the dead cast
myself into the waves preferring to drown
rather than arrive

eyes breasts fingers navel cunt asshole
tomorrow I just want to sleep and never
wake up guiltless my prick enters her
while I'm dreaming so I'm not responsible
for the sacrament of sex or orgasm or
companionship it's always the same dream
mothercold eyes or piano keys I'd like to
press to become one of those people who
carry love inside them all the time

fold back on the edges of a blind eye a memory of the future a dismantling and rewelding of the English language

in one Shakespearean breath like the ocean of a prelude something you draw back deep into the throat and lungs

in the multiplicity of what we love and what loves us each piece of a never-rising sun assembled in the dark until it's motionless a first dawning a second light a shining close to forgiveness

shakti shakti mother of space unbecoming unborn unmade unformed

sunshredded flameform nestled under the covers the sound of our laughter wakes us up

night shining through the brutally poetic years of being alone that both of us endured or enjoyed ecstatically before we met each other the window's open slightly I hear voices outside I'm always slightly surprised that I have not died in my sleep

sorrow of a last breath no way for birdsign

or sacrifice to ward off the sombre grace of
the dawn

axle glowing in the socket throw back your
veils set me on the way of the goddess who
with her own hands conducts the man who
knows through all things

axons return to their resting places in my
nervous system like stars to their orbits

language is a punishment a terrible secret
a sign of enormous guilt which comes
through like a police siren or a motet-voice
in rotation but I'll tell you how the sun rose
one ribbon at a time

perpetually unfolding inwardness like silks
pulled from a magician's sleeve waves of
scent her pelvis falling like water from a
fountain light from the bodega across the
street keeps us

awake stamp her eyes with Ariel-charms the
wind in our flesh our voices like characters
in a play of silence

often wake up sobbing rolling from dream
to dream hungover begin to relax only once

I start drinking uncomfortable with how much people trust me I always suspect I'm going to fuck it up or betray them I'm not sure why it's an ordinary fear

losing people losing yourself losing your breath that creates the atmosphere great chunks of conscious intention break off from the glacier you're so unhappy N says kissing my neck my cheek my chest stroking my hair I feel like you don't want to be here

can't account for the terror inside of language can't wrest a last work of ferocious beauty from the depths of futility and despair a book should grieve us deeply like a banishment

watch the birds in the blue daybreak I dreamed I was castrated but I can't say by whom

curb my desires as a measure of self-protection at the resurrection they'll prop us up and put us back in line for more scalding tears the wheel dark turns living in this narrow band of sensitivity the parameters of which I obey like yellow lines on the highway plan to live separately when our lease ends like people who move upstream from the river they polluted

feelings lost like decibels in the ear still alive well-tended and shiny like a new toy lost and comfortless fill clear mason jar drinking six cups every morning nettle infusion on the counter rye bread slathered with honey

dirty windows soon scratchy throat remnants of energy despite the failed hypothesis of sleep like the sharp cry of a bird when it sees the bed stripped of its nestlings I say the word love even when I don't mean it better to abort the lining of the womb N keeps talking about the child we gave up lips glued together quick desire each shadow makes her stop each murmur stay

crossfire of images continually running away from the subject greasy smells from the kitchen do you want me to fry up an egg Mom would always ask me on Sunday mornings while Dad read the paper on his lap a pot of coffee on the table have to fart keep it trapped beneath the covers don't move no pry my mouth open with your fingers force your words down my throat sample my abandonment

eruption of exhausted karma biting her thighs licking along her navel innocent plain-faced dominant we become carnal through scratching teasing laughing fighting

Satie-scales while it rains smear cold cream under the eyes erase the crinkle of last night's sorrow I've heard it all before how the day begins touch me completely with flowers

coconut oil cut tulips weak old sweat burned into the sheets on some level I want her to be a boy and she wants me to be a woman

my back hurts so much just getting older twist the clitoris stem prolong the climax at the end shit fuck me slender clumsy body still half asleep love stories

love letters love of life it's irreducible to further description like a map of purgatory stick your cock in my ass she begs the hands gripping her little hips I want to feel you deep it's a bad sign that I don't love anyone in the present tense I'm always looking back

take the dominant role in bed it seems like I can't meet a woman who doesn't like being choked and slapped called demeaning names reduced to the ashes of meaning two people going to the bottom of a river one falling and the other diving

lingerie the aroma of soap don't know at all what it's like to be alone anymore I've discovered it's almost impossible my personality is a cavity which must be filled but no one's keeping score this self-excoriation adds up to nothing

plagues storms wars are products of the same blind force which operate in microbes wash the shit off my cock rub soap over my scrotum while she sits on the toilet expelling the semen from her rectum it's not vulgar at all just the damage that the soul must endure on its way to becoming real

a haze of bacteria hovers above over every object a thick cloud of cells my toothbrush is not sanitary need to change the sheets

the tip of my penis hurts just a little bit I
wonder if I have an STI

turn the page like a knife in the wound

towel off where are her fingers rain echoing
arpeggios stroke the curls at her cunt earth
and salt shave her legs like wheat

thrown back on my own defenses
remorselessly like a fox smoked out and
driven into a clearing put another record
on the sun lets down its hair Dante chants
along the grassy slopes of Mount Purgatory
I cry like I almost always do listening to
Carrie & Lowell so few things make me
feel emotion anymore it's concerning the
sign and body of a lost presence I was born
aware of mortality like a car built to run in
reverse

enter into the state that words want to create
in me like a nervous breakdown traced
across the page dismantling the regime of
representation working on a novel about
the last hours of Paul Celan before he threw
himself into the Seine

wandering marked signified drowned

like a nail's been driven through my feet I
cannot walk towards him

the difficulty of bearing witness engenders
the need

like in the Vedas logos shattered a planetary
body dispersed across great gaps of sorrow
there's something luminous and unsettling
trapped behind our words in the poems we
released like doves

so full of excuses each day begins without
a plan read about sports in my phone try
to arrange sex outside the boundaries
of my relationship entangle myself in
this electronic matrix of disappointment
deception despair derangement deviance
glances stolen like fruit from the trees
objectloss is transformed into egoloss the
heart that does not leap becomes its own
obstacle an amorphous free-floating mass
of stale romantic despair the curtains stayed
closed the condition of Saturn's children
becomes ambiguous

it's Good Friday today I've started to put
on my running gear knees hurt a little along

the sides almost as if someone is pressing on them with the palms of their hands grief is akin to swelling around the joint our inborn defense system localizes the point of pain and immobilizes it

like a hot air balloon passing over farmland or a lake in a desert where birds land under the moon an archaic power that renders itself intelligible to itself

purely oral vocal and musical my breath the sound of my footfalls the cry of birds the hum of traffic the splatter of intermittent rainfall and birdsong

toe-shoes feel soggy my calves are tight have I hydrated enough should be drinking more bone-broth tendonitis in my Achilles might snap at any moment the brain is an inference engine that seeks to minimize prediction and error freewill is a phantom limb the free energy principle tries to explain how biological systems maintain their order by restricting themselves to a limited number of states

a sequence of jolting aesthetic breakthroughs

scissor the soul into slender strips

the wings of butterflies climb the dogwood
tree and the playgym while Mom chats in
the alley with Marge the neighbor my sister
lays in the grass I am four years old a skull
a dreamer asleep in a cave in the dark my
sister will have children one day it's bizarre
that someone else comes buys a house raises
a family in it starts the cycle over homes
should be turned into cemeteries when a
family's done with them like the way coral
reefs are built out of dead exoskeletons in
the future billions of people will no longer
exist

dogwood blossoms fall pink and white
across the lawn

still have a shard of glass in my foot from
the other night when I stumbled into the
kitchen to get water knocked a mason jar
off the counter didn't sweep it all up the
run itself is straight down MacDonough
until I hit Nostrand an eerie link appears to
exist between entangled particles when you
still love someone you hope they can hear
your thoughts like a radio signal I'd have

married you even though it wouldn't have worked my memory doesn't quite feel intact things are missing or loosened the raw voice angles higher and higher rejoice rejoice at halfspeed I'm not taking any pleasure in what I'm doing most people are frightened of becoming dependent on their subjectivity in the montage at the end of the film the mother character says that if you don't love your life will pass by you in a flash

out of breath calves aching blood pumping through my brain jump to the top of the porch enter the keycode run up the stairs push open the left-open door hair's damp pull off my toe-shoes

examine myself in the mirror for probably five or ten minutes every morning there is no past only the future in disguise

at the margins of self-betrayal

boring predictable airtight self-love seeks only its own sophisticated pleasures grab a towel start the shower start the electric tea kettle plug in the coffeegrinder take the jar of beans down from the shelf

grind the beans pour the water into the
French press stir what goes in the smoothie
frozen blueberries bananas raw milk raw
honey spirulina three raw eggs took a long
bath last night practically fell asleep because
of the heat and the odor of Eucalyptus in
the back of my skull there's a tape of my
whole life play the whole thing from start
to finish I wonder if that's heaven or hell
I've tricked myself into believing in healthy
food and exercise and this cabinet full of
supplements look like agony today shaved
last night need to shower again pour gobs
of body wash into my hands lather my groin
my armpits my asshole look into the mirror

brush the hair away from my eyes back
towards the top of my skull my own
insecurity prevents me from doing anything
that would expose me too much self-care
is about getting our bodies back into the
competitive marketplace

isolated thoughts can't form metaphors
remain inert like gas unconscious wishes
stop striving to get themselves satisfied
feel so clean after my shower we're too

emotional or not emotional enough awake
she's poured the coffee mixed it with butter
and cream and honey puts the cup in my
hands says drink she's memorizing lines for
Hamlet on the floor you need to breathe
she says putting her hand on my chest you
don't breathe enough

condensed painless intimacy like a corpse
trapped beneath a frozen river hands pressed
against the ice I do everything but care for
the person who cares for me a wounded
animal that's dragged itself into the corner
of its den love is the basic force in a world
of primitive mental forces the higher levels
of organization do terrifying and shocking
and surprising things in the course of the
meandering stream of narration like a cloud
at sea it's actual torture the violence of the
withheld harmonies the coldness of Mahler's
dissonance on record our apartment is full
of the books we read constantly which keeps
us together reading is the only vice that
adequately replaces all other vices

longjohns wool socks green trousers a
turtleneck and a blue sweater it's still pretty

chilly outside but I'll probably get warm when I'm indoors

a storm of words a deathstyle on my typewriter nothing permanent is old only mortal things fail to renew themselves lose their elasticity and youth when the Eagles lost Dad and I would be in a black mood for hours or days children are right about the absoluteness with which they adore and cling to things just as my fingers make music they make innocence

what I think and what I want and how I live are all different things on different tracks but I think you made me pity you out of instinct which is something N has never done half-naked I traced your bones like leaves stopped short of telling you about the contradictions which seemed so sensual at the time like in the winter when the heat kicks on and bodies grow warm like houses an organism only wishes to die after its own fashion scattering the light I carry into the poetic reality of substitution this collection of atoms strains to be melded with that collection of atoms I took you for granted

I take everyone for granted only the strong ones break away from me so I commend you the whole city circulates and breathes like a set of lungs N asks what I'm writing I say the same old thing

a second self carries all the hurt my letters and journals are kept under my bed we extend beyond our bodies we're more interesting enmeshed in a network of relationships the plumber was supposed to come yesterday but he never showed up our old roommates were very bland smoked watched TV all day there was a time when my family still got together to actually talk around a table Mom shut off early in childhood Dad always stood up for her that's what he signed up for

my sister stays cut off utterly abandoned in a senseless universe without countries or borders we exist in a vast zone of annihilation of which the earth is merely a subregion a tiny pinprick unlovingly made in the dark go through long stretches of perfect health punctuated by terrible fevers and chills maybe twice a year almost like clockwork I'm not built for a good death

fathers and sons postpone their relationship
until it's too late Dad leaned forward told
me that I had been a good son I couldn't
bear it a nerve compressed in my neck
sends pain everywhere like the spider plant
climbing up the window what happens

when you break self-wounding words apart
do they catch fire N says the play she's
writing has to do with her sister and a snake
my mood has infected hers and I know it's
not fair but I can't seem to live without a
woman propping me up I'm very subtle and
extremely pragmatic about getting what
I want should we make eggies touch her
forehead with my finger

place healing flowers on the ulcer of my
mouth the record's skipping a relationship
is really the misunderstandings that
accumulate around an erotic bond rub N's
wrist I tell her I care about her

start to put my shoes on to go

you're not listening you think I'm melting
with tenderness when you walk in the room

but that's only because you're a narcissist who can't imagine that people do anything around you other than melt with tenderness she says while I don't look back

the wind

runs its hands through the grass the world with its remorseless logic pushes me forward towards the aboveground J

the tape is running I lie to myself can't catch the slip-ups can't hear them I need someone else to be objective for me

pull the nerves out of my brain like angelhair pasta in grad school I lived in an old house that spooked me and shuddered on windy nights my friends would visit from the city we would stay up late drinking and talking it was very jovial I would throw parties my sister would drunkenly make espresso the future is promiscuous gets down on its hands and knees I never go to see a therapist a part of me really fears what would happen if I opened up

a long process of compression

train time is hyperfluid hyper-relative sleep-
starved each day blurs at the edges of the
last once this island was just trees before we
encouraged its destruction into this daily
regime of ugliness waste and fraud I eat
goji berries from a bag in my jacket pocket
watch the reflections of other travelers in
the mirror that was a bad email I wrote
last night violating the instructions I gave
Orpheus transforms the natural world with
a surging wave of interdiction the poetic
process is grounded in the erotic events

numbly processing information the way
a lizard takes in sunlight so much of any
single day is governed by biological needs
economic needs psychological needs we're
constantly alchemizing our leisure time into
productive time ate too much yesterday
felt bloated all day smoked salmon and
cottage cheese and eggs with rye-bread
a man in a green coat is asleep and smells
like vinegar nobody sits near him held
here because of train traffic ahead of us we
should be moving shortly headphones block
sound screens absorb light and interest
the earth's eyes have gone blind when the

telegraph was invented in the nineteenth century information could be transmitted at the rate of about four bits per second we're maladapted to the evolving forces of an imminent future farming has become a hybrid of factory production and mining its waste becomes a pollutant poisoning waterways and aquifers pathos leaks out forms new landmasses islands continents chokes the air with fumes remakes the earth the soul begins in the womb and continues to grow after our death like hair I can't read a book for longer than a few minutes more and more the texture of physical resembles a digital environment have to switch at Fulton

to the 4 the connective tissue of each day is simply waiting I carry a little book on ancient Greek in my pocket which I tell myself that I'm supposed to read while I wait on the platform

immersed in the ephemeral nature of the digital newspaper the dialectical image of the self-updating perpetual icon of a world vanishing

the mind can't get into a flow state anymore
Augustine says multiply your imagination
like the light of the sun make it greater or
brighter as you will the morphological and
ideological ironies are acute

impulses are metronomic the subway
system is a vascular and alive sloppily
shunting us around the body politic spent
too much money last weekend at Olmsted
for a friend's birthday it has nothing to
do with emotional or physical satiety just
fake finery and masturbatory dishes so that
you're obligated to leave a fat tip

shut the book like eyelids

off the train it's a luminous morning in Grand
Central station under vaulted and artificial
stars I suddenly felt like walking around I
like it here it was five years ago almost to
the day that I waited for your train to pull
in you were still in college I couldn't pick
you out of the crowd so I had to call but you
were right there the age difference doesn't
seem like a big deal now but it was when
you were eighteen we were house sitting
that weekend for my friend it was perfect

but I'm idealizing it now because I don't like the way my life's turned out I gave you my book to read Sonata you said it was too close to us and you were right as if I'd written you into existence the day was still young we decided to stay inside a pair of loonies who complain that the noose is too tight while pulling it tighter and tighter you're napping in the other room not defeated or hostile just exhausted the walls float luminous as daybreak oceanic like silence in motion my college band sucked I found it embarrassing to perform at those shitty house parties wake up the next day a little wine drunk the difference between a child and an adult is that an adult can provide their own security Mom sings Edelweiss she wheels me in the shopping cart we're going to get groceries together it's obvious from the drop off in my journal entries that I'm losing the ability to be alone like a deserter floating through a neutral country a cigarette clutched between his teeth

split myself into female and male parts cut a furrow in the self plant new sacred groves a nervous system requires so much energy that's why we need tools to help us the last time she came over we drank coffee and listened to Schubert and cried about her breakup Eda really wants to have children

descend

to the subway again head uptown

wrist hurts getting carpal-tunnel fried the power in the kitchen yesterday didn't realize what was happening for an hour thought I was going to lose my mind until I tried flipping the breaker soul-making is a process of de-automatization a mother of four young kids steps onto the train yells at them to be quiet and then opens her phone as they wriggle next to her ignored

eyeless onlookers clouds grey bundles of perception drifting by

in a few generations will anyone ever contemplate these things again the inexplicable lives we cling to hoping for meaning

beauty has been driven into the hills by efficiency get water get food get sex full of cynical hope only behave this way because I have an average-sized cock I wouldn't try so hard otherwise gave N herpes last year from eating her out how could I be so stupid when I had something on my lip neither of us were thinking clearly there are no hierarchies a mineral is equal to an angel or an apple everything is made up of the indestructible light of beginning it's fractals from top to bottom like paths that form on the lawn of a college campus after thousands of students have taken a shortcut it's much better to recognize that we live amidst confusion and idealized images Socrates doubted that a person was a human being at birth it doesn't come so easy and neither does knowledge like a star deep in a far off galaxy its light just now arriving

the cancer's not being killed is it helping Dad fix the fence along the alley we removed the sections in strips his arms and neck were tan from days working in the sun he seemed happy

a form of gnosis that gathers the moment in like a harvest

stalled halfway to the next station a heap
of cinders holding violent feelings in
melancholics live in the same world as other
people yet they do not see the same world
they build themselves a new world into
which they alone can enter

shame about the way the dying piss and
shit themselves those under the influence
of Saturn can tell the future but they can't
share it with anyone the heart's silence is
a zero sum game Dad and Calvin could
walk for miles and miles for thirteen years
together I was so devastated when the dog
was put down cried on the floor of my
apartment when I heard the news a panic
attack

begins out of nowhere like a wave on
lake hiding inside the smallest particles
of matter I close my eyes I wonder if I'm
imagining all this or if I'm still under the
covers a sleeping giant in a cave

get off at 86th walk west

escape

the sky torn open by the souls of the dead on

their way to heaven letting the rain through
drowned pale and twisted in the mud

a girl on her way to school tosses her hair
back in exultation against the rain saw the
circling birds years lost in the middle of
teaching which I despised particularly the
debasement of my intelligence and seeing
you for the last time ripped something open
a seal I don't know why I keep thinking of
you

you don't think about me

at the Neue Gallery at the corner of 86th
and Fifth drink the last of my water bottle
before they make me throw it away through
a metal-detector get a free entry pin from
my friend who works the coat-check all the
employees are attractive in a very curated
way

through a pinhole of light

a large poplar at dusk with a gathering
storm behind it

the eye is a great heart that sends the
paintbrush hurling lavish gold gown

filigreed with ovoid shapes eyes eggs fish blended into a golden background of circles spirals and squares Klimt was fascinated with cells with sperm and eggs on the other side of the column

a nude female floats forward at her feet an infant lies wrapped in a swath of tulle the face is the most important visual image we ever encounter

sky water trees sails houses no two of these things are treated in the same way the brushstrokes adjust to the visual impression made by the object in the domain of light in college I lived across from an old Linden tree that was home to hundreds of blackbirds in the winter I always felt like they were watching me through the window I was on the fourth floor and addressed them at eye-level sincerity is not to be found outside the realm of grief in a tide of stones thin strokes no longer separate or distinct the voice says not to stand too close to the paintings shimmering patterns abstract compositions unstable dynamic transformational

hands-with-phones like Octopus tentacles

with ten thousand neurons apiece extending
the brain beyond the brain a polluted mind
develops deadzones like an ocean Celan
touched his father's hands through the
chainlink fence of the concentration camp
the gas-chambers smelled of almonds

white face pink cheeks big oval eyes strands
of hair drape down from each side of her
neck and blend with the gold of her dress
we drove to Maine the summer I was ten
Mom had a panic attack we didn't swim it
was too cold later the doctor prescribed her
Klonopin for anxiety it affected her memory
for years

there are these shifts

that as children we don't perceive logically
like the subtle movement between seasons
every step along the way our neural circuits
are rewiring visual images but the bottom-
up process alone can't resolve the anarchy of
information

watercolor and pastel applied wet on cream
paper fish-glue and a finish of whitening
small beech trees in the sun with a few

conifers mixed in the autumn Dad got sick and lost all that weight Mom stopped sleeping I let death pass around me like a storm it's remarkable that the laws of nature we find on this planet apply all the way out to the edge of the universe the slender trunks of the poplars form a tenuous curtain of waving leafage I feel their tangible presence violet countryside red rivers black streams green and yellow women blue children wild poppies the natural world is morally restorative Klimt lures you barefooted into the garden laughing

down the stairs to the adjacent cafe take a seat order espresso listen to the pianist and the chatter of old people rain and traffic animals grieve they nudge corpses as if they would reanimate nature's not figured out what to do with its excess feelings hospital food has no nutritional value jello and bread my eyes hurt from overwork I always get so exhausted at museums the expenditure of energy is always so much greater than I anticipate

brush the hair from my eyes sip the

bitter espresso feel the rumblings of hunger ignore them I like this strung out caffeinated feeling start to write you a letter in my notebook but I don't have your address you are free to see me as you like including as a manipulative person and to see this exchange as just another iteration of manipulation given the coming to light of certain reprehensible aspects of my past and indeed my character mark it carefully in blue pencil and tell me the pages you want changed if you think it comes too close to the way things actually were each little bit is a thought not a bare idea or opinion or lesson which comes from the flesh of the head with instinct running through it like a countermelody a form of expression that neither expresses anything in the world or the self a vomiting of one's whole being

exploit the empty circle of my capacities before I run out of juice I'm beginning to feel desperate enough to write something but will you read it little moments accumulate and accumulate this is an act of time travel I'm reaching my hand out can you shake it I want to cry entropy breaks everything down you're there among the cargo of the dead packed away I receive you with unresurrecting hands afraid that at some point the emotion will dry up inside the shell I've constructed around it

the way most if not all your work is written reflects a high degree of neurosis N said reading the manuscript

flashes of a recognizable personality something that gets systemized or becomes almost rote like a textbook

a word hardly spoken loses its meaning like muscle flesh created for the fall calves still tight massage them under the table general soreness the tendon stretched taut like a suspension bridge my back hurts too near the shoulders and the base of the spine dust rises from the tables like the ashes from a burnt-out city the tissue of the soul's exposed like ligaments in a war-wound

toddling across the blue carpet Dad has the camera Mom's got curls still down to her shoulders she was insecure about her looks I undervalued Dad's friendship he never asked anything of me except trust

free-will like a phantom limb searching for moral compensation burrow into my notebook find a more flexible path there's symmetry everywhere secreting no sign of a masterpiece

elliptical and undiscerning from the lowest levels of organic material up through to language and literature there are scripts and interpretations of scripts which twist back and talk to themselves

take a sip of espresso so bitter scratch the side of my head stretch my legs out under the table scribble arabesques to encourage the pen to give more ink art rejects its own beginnings conceals them the way a bird protects its nest or flees from it at the first sign of a predator writings choke out real physical life take over the garden plot style is the manifold of opposites that must be kept together

egocide fear of how sex with a man would change me I like watching two women have sex while I watch maybe that's unfair or

cowardly it's like I'm always advising others
to break the taboos I can't break for myself
go piss downstairs open Tinder on my phone
with one hand pee with another smooth out
the wrinkles in my corduroys brush my hair
with my wet hand don't really know what
emotions would mean if they didn't mean
suffering the fluorescent lights around the
mirrors bring out all my wrinkles and lines
I'm getting old faster than I'd like to admit
I lack exposure to my own perilous capacity
for self-obliteration

foreshadowing all that will come the last
act the great exhalation the weight of time
returning

just let it breathe and expand first

on a blue morning Pop-Pop ambled about
the mountains we made a fire in the stone
fireplace he built by hand just like that
when I was four I could feel my heartbeat
I was afraid it would stop beating if I
thought about it too much a billion years
of evolution for the sake of one more day
the earth is a feedback loop an existential
Internet went and bought books for N

yesterday after we got in a fight on the street and I didn't say goodbye and neither did she more cunnelingus lately but that has more to do with compensating for my dwindling erections ask for the bill take out my credit card wait patiently for the waiter to return contemplate the tip

emotions bubble up from the deepest substrate

eyes dim like the sea in winter an act of collusion against the framework of the self imagine how my life would have turned out if you had been there waiting at the airport

laid on the ground with my phone next to my ear waiting for you to say something all I could hear was static but I knew you were there the pattern is confounding say thank you take my raincoat from the coat-rack eyes downcast avoidant like someone in the dark with their hands tied behind their backs hauling themselves forward with their teeth still drizzling

damp hair damp shoes the rain makes everything look incredibly green tomorrow

afterschool on Fridays I would walk five
blocks to Mr. Heffner's little house for
piano lessons

still alive regret never going back to see him

horizontally and vertically the space of a
single day stretches back and forth dips into
past-futures and future-pasts present-pasts
and past-presents

south on Park heading towards The Met
on 84th heart draining out endlessly like a
broken bucket Empedocles believed that the
cosmos is perpetually inhaling and exhaling
the breath of desire she came over for tea
I fingered her a little and she put her head
on my shoulder that was last winter she left
I cried for some reason what was her name
I'm prepared at all times for terrible shocks
the future deforms the present like a metal
sheet warped by a powerful magnet

toes squilch in my boots there's water on my
glasses what a mess

up

the stairs flanked on either side by newly

constructed fountains through security
check my bag and raincoat hold onto my
notebook past the Roman columns through
the Great Hall

shoe sounds kids on school tours art
students with roving eyes elderly folks
moving slowly tourists and their families
dragging each other along

straight ahead to Medieval Art small black
shadows dapple the ground I follow the
shining pathway of the sun like waterplants
on a river an early unfolding lilac head
through the railings of a suburban garden
maybe each universe is just a single cell
jostling for space in an infinite vacuum like
the Diamond Sutra tell us Mary's clothed in
a blue a hard-to-acquire and valuable color
when I was six Mom let me have all the ice
cream I wanted after I lost my two front
teeth pranced around the house showing
off for everyone stuck out my tongue what
depth of feeling comes into being because
of a window instead of letting the Christ-
child look at him the artist makes him turn
out of the picture revealing a stratum of

secret pain an abscess that pours out and
drains away aureoled in light

what right do I have to complain about
suffering I was dust and ash I was nothing

again a monologue of twoness black flies
circle my father's body like gawkers after
creation God sat on his haunches eating the
placenta of darkness licking his paws

extinguished incense and rain remnants of
time the tombs on the floors of churches
bore basrelief effigies of the buried I didn't
go to the funeral after X shot himself all my
friends were there but they were too polite
to question my excuse

slowly dismantling the self until all that's
left are beams and rafters

concentric circles of enervated light

at the first division of the canto the belt loop
fell around your neck I dragged you to the
floor of the big room with quiet windows in
the dark

on the second floor

embarking on his daily course across the sky Apollo symbolizes the planets an allegorical figures on the cornice represents the four continents plated Mars bends like a silhouette in imitation silk empty hands turned to the falling west

Titian's early landscapes lie in the no-man's-land between the sacred and the profane I stopped seeing your face after a few years and not even photography allows these paralyzed moments to cross the room and reach you

disgust signals which animal should be peeled off from the herd there's never really any release in the hypersexual city it's just constant jacking off without cumming it would be better to throw it all overboard every nerve in the body and just float without feeling anything I turned my life into the subject of books I am all these other people and they are me different layers of my personality confront themselves as if multiple fats have dissolved in a hot liquid floating in competing globules on the surface behind the horizon of time

dream after dream out of sequence born
blue choked for oxygen

drowsy because I don't sleep properly often
wake up gasping for air heart pounding I'm
not getting enough oxygen probably

deviated septum need more coffee anxiety
is a market demand the higher the cost
of pleasure the lower the quality of life
the more degraded the civilization spend
evenings watching basketball on my laptop
at Whole Foods eating a salad using the free
Wi-Fi

he was proud of me but what do I care
why does it matter the three of us isolated
him within the family structure that's the
mother's prerogative he lived in the same
town his whole life knew every road and
backroad would ride his bike every dark
every night as a kid I never met his mother
because she died young my parents had
kids so that they could stop grieving for
their childhoods which is why I can't have
children right now

because I still feel like their kid

a reference to the things that forgetfulness
has not yet absorbed or buried

kept habits from my father as a way of
protecting him from my indifference

emotive effect of flaming light or actual
flames seems to have been discovered in the
late 1490's Bellini used sunset and sunrise
to heighten the mood of his pictures we
owe much of our pleasure in looking at
the world to the great artists who have
come before us the lyric voice starts from
nowhere like a wind at sea and to Leonardo
a human being was part of a vast machine
to be understood part by part he dissected
and anatomized the female body removed
its mystery unstringing muscles detaching
bones even cracking open wombs the eye
instinctively looks for analogies at the basic
level of organization we behave like lichen
clinging to a tree energy's pure hiding place

a     self-organisatizing     self-assembling
pattern from free energy mind emerges
like storm from a cloudsystem I never
walk around with headphones don't want
to live in an artificial mood the Virgin of

the Rocks plays a long sonata of the dead
painting is transformed by the way we
receive it technology is a virus a self-
replicating decentralized invisible mode of
anti-life because even if our current mode
of living doesn't destroy the human race it
will destroy the human spirit we've lost the
distinction between the hand and the tool
on Instagram everything's sun-drained and
choppy everyone's smiling some teenage
bitch takes selfies weirdly deluded people
scurry back and forth across the European
wing like gusts of fog

returning to the old masters is an act of
self-making a restoration of the trauma of
modernity the restoration of the nature
which Shakespeare worked into the tissue
of language thereby naturalizing it

beyond the threshold of lingering memory
kissed the paleness inside you and licked
your bones clean

in limbo with the voices of the dumb and
blind small distinct comma-like brushstrokes
break the surface into vibrating packets the
brush registers the fleeting effects of sunset

and finds the angel of atmospheric pressure nature loses its aliveness and yet gains the metaphorical intensity of expanding relative time in my dream Dad bled into the shaving bowl like his throat was cut and I stood there impassive like I was listening to a secret in another ten years I'll become that guy having a midlife crisis at a bar trying to talk to younger women I'm forced to reject most of what I discover about myself in Dante the crater is the pit from which stars become visible by daylight

grief's recorded in the geology of the soul go down far enough layers track the record of every shock and trauma boys learn self-consciously to walk and talk in certain ways like athletes or rock stars even but it leaves them crippled I was afraid that my parents would die from a very young age watched with horror as it come into view slowly over the course of many years Mom in certain fundamental ways chose to pathologize her daughter rather than face her so the pattern is that I've run away from people like sunlight across a lawn

esoteric time is measured by the thick knots
in the brain like rings in a tree human
nature is a resurrection all the time skipped-
stones sucked into the mud of a dried-up
river at sunrise Monet was scrupulous about
the linear structure of his compositions
journeying up and down the Seine Valley
and the channel coast he settled for good at
Giverny midway between Paris and Rouen
no painter has ever been more sensitive to
the anatomy of time and place none has
ever more feelingly evoked the sweep and
respiration of space nature's secret heartbeat
keenly alive to the luminosity of the skies
a composition in the Japanese manner
plunging glimpses of the sea viewed from a
foreground of cliffs a dazzling flood

water with weeds waving at the bottom

my sister and I hunt for Easter eggs I've
watched the old tapes a dozen times I start
to cry immediately had a party last week at
our apartment our friends leafed through
our books played our records actors from
the play I wrote were there I guess because
they want me to write another role for them

none of it seems real apartment subway job
dinner drinks socializing of all kinds going
to the theater taking in concerts being
entertained as a kid I forced myself not
to cry little ones grow up to take revenge
on the behavior of the big people who rule
them like a machine producing loaves of
bread or silicon chips or steel a conveyor
belt leads from my brain to my mouth
skips the heart leaves me desperate we're
expected to be able to perform drone roles
inside a monstrously complicated system
it's no wonder we break down and don't
show up to work acquire more houseplants
get nice furniture get rid of everything
plastic our apartment is a mess the process
of uglification has been underway for a few
hundred years black branches the earth calls
us back like children returning home in the
dusk

winter thawing outside like rhythmic splice-
up footage

as mysterious as the work of magnets the
gleaners carry the sunlight with them on
their backs

a ballpoint pen creates a dense network of
color with circular movements on polyester
canvas equally reminiscent of both sky and
sea pain oozes up from the floors like oil
or mud I think of the significance of the
time I wasted from lethargy or fear women
wash their linens in the river meadows roll
back towards the edge of the picture and
seemingly forever only a saint could be as
united with his God as Cézanne was with
his work the beautiful is a manifestation
of secret laws of nature which would have
remained hidden a Cezanne flower is aural
a language of violence and kinetic searching
each painting contains is a superabundance
of reality an escape from this sense of failure
and the disarray and constant humiliation
what's remarkable is not how clearly or
powerfully we remember childhood but how
little of it remains intact if anything it's all
conjecture and fictionalizing reconstruction
am I happy to be alive

all becomes clear and simple when one opens
an eye within life grieves for itself Mom
hangs Christmas decorations Nat King Cole
on the stereo Dad brings up more boxes of

decorations from the basement my sister dances we bundle the dead off into eternity like sending garbage to a landfill the frame will only be felt as a vague interpretation of whatever is perceived within it attention directs us to the object the enigma in the foreground

a series of balanced lines the incandescence of the sea light wild roses and knifegrass exposed lemon yellows then unexpectedly a field of poppies

the curving lines coincide within the figurative complexity of my language I don't understand the rich texture of motives inside me if a tree is turned upside down with its roots in the air the roots become leaves and buds two gigantic spiral nebulae twine around each other eleven enormously enlarged stars with aureoles stark blue sky staggering in turmoil six billion years has been rearranged into me

four cut sunflowers 1887

peach trees merciful cream colored buds breaking into a half-fearful almost religious background of blue and white the countryside is dying

just touch the mouth touch the eyes quiet mute gestures of despair a simple gesture indicating a divided self

always roots seeking earth we're too emotional or not emotional enough

falling spears of color pierce me through the forehead

dirty yellow and shimmering blue the heart itself with storms and tides and depths and pearls

such a great fire in the soul and yet nobody ever comes to warm themselves from the surface volcanic islands formed from eruptions in chaos color radiates from the center of the painting like a chain of quasars I write the same book over and over again the one about the shape the voice takes when it longs for the edges of speech Celan was a poet who could only write in fragments some guy with big coke bottle glasses is breathing heavily sniffling like his nose is blocked missed a little bit of my neck shaving pluck

the hairs out with my fingers my eyes hurt I
need a new prescription the vertical format
of the picture gives prominence to the lilies

take the sweater off

my feet are sweaty Renoir would walk
from town to town painting when he was
a young man he resented the express trains
for turning people into anonymous and
passive passengers words sieve and strain
reality but never imprison it from the
vantage of the past or the future our present
is an unenviable one a web of mantra-like
punishments

wheatfields in dry heat he paints with his
eyes closed rolling hills olive-toned girls
in white dresses walk down to the sea my
ancestors grew large and heavy and split off
to America like seeds caught in the wind
nothing we felt was disconnected from what
the earth was feeling my mother has joined
the ranks of the very lonely if the fire in the
hearth goes out the family is put at risk the
fire must be tended to I'm upstairs in my
room drinking green tea I was depressed
that whole summer when I read the first

volume of Beckett's lightblue letters

quickly a hummingbird flies through a crack in the wall Mom chops vegetables for dinner Dad watches baseball the smell of laundry Eda sings in her room I thought love could keep people alive forever I performed all sorts of rituals to ensure it

light of the sun I close my mouth around her nipple draw nourishment I've been alive for ten days or more everything is a blur I grew up with the dread of being uglier than them

from far enough away you see everything clearly the rest of your life distance is equivalent to truth the spring is fading already before winter is over the future decays into the present like a corpse rotting in the sun I'm four years old in the backyard with my sister slopping watercolors across a piece of butcher paper now Eda lives on a farm with cows and dogs and cats and geese she says everything she eats is the best thing she's ever had human beings have destroyed the greatest gift of all their connection with nature

openly weeping now like I'm at a wedding
this is the first spring without my father
I'm not ready to be the only one responsible
for myself affection is how the middle-class
express their feelings that's why affection
comes in gestures

divided interrupted broken off from itself
a bulwark of the purest most perfect
awareness a small bird will drop dead from
a bough without ever having felt sorry for
itself

unduly elliptic drawn from some ever less
public ever more intimate part of myself
such inertia and void as never before we
are annihilated light scattered apeiron or
the indistinct Anaximander calls it the basic
grammar of the world tomatoes and peppers
and kale and parsley and mint in the garden
the dog died first then everything fell apart
strangely it was the autumn they both
stopped walking the TV spent never got
turned off colony collapse more and more
my own language appears to me like a veil
that must be torn apart in order to get at
the nothingness behind it

the greater pattern is seen and can emerge
the tally of these choral effects a series
of fires far off in the dark perforated in a
million places as You pour into us like blood

hollowbright corona emanate I cry out from
the flowing rock

disciplining myself just so that I can feel
something other than this addicted need for
stimulus like everyone else we're truly in a
hell of our own creation

high blood pressure she's on a low dose of
medication the doctor says it causes the
heart walls to thicken I think if Mom died
I'd die too

avoid conversation partly out of discomfort
partly out of contempt for the both of us

dogwood blossoms fall pink and white
across the lawn

what happens after we die if not nothing

how deeply human it was to be their
child how lovingly Dad took home videos
transferring them from tape to digital in the

year before he died

keep my emotions silent which is how I kill
them feet hurt just want to sit down my
mother smelled her father's cigarettes on
the porch at the beach house a few weeks
after he died white billowing clouds roll
over the park the sun falls west fragments
of seamusic Turner echo mist and water the
search is not a linear it's a polyvalent thread
which stretches beneath the surface linking
ideas together under its own subtle logic
long image-chains assemble layers form
the fishermen carry the drowned man back
to shore there's no moral truth only moral
style in his late plays Shakespeare begins to
develop a new kind of magic that is neither
pagan nor Christian a magic of enchanted
grief Schubert on his deathbed began to
talk about utterly new harmonies but we
never got to hear them

blindness is a recurrent theme the high
collar of his buttoned up great-coat
aggravates the loneliness emanating from
the canvas the old man's elongated limbs
and cramped angular posture recall El

Greco bare consciousness like an old coin that has fallen out of circulation the bulk of self-observation remains latent in the background lurking like an animal in its den teeth bared eyes shining his face icy bluish-white his coat a deep cobalt his eyes wells of navy a blue bullet hole on his subject's temple lays the tragedy bare

exhaust myself in the search for you this fragment city green edges of wet light passing through the glass overhead

riverbirds scutter above the atrium and circle downward along the park I catch the eyeballs of tourist girls dark almond eyes jazz lips a sense of dirtiness hurried organisms gentle genital convulsions no one can see what I'm thinking bored meaningless empty sexual thoughts about people I can't possibly care about my novels appear to be very different but they can in fact be seen as entangled roots a voice in very brief dream-monologues gathered into an imperfect composite through the gazes and voices of those around it a confused feedback loop that can't pick a signal out of its own noise my intellectual life coruscates sparking here and there like a firefly on the porch but illuminating nothing for long a flowchart of pictures and words stripped of nostalgia the stakes of the old house will be pulled up like thick weeds I'm wearing a baseball jersey Dad has a beer the Phillies game is on the radio I've just gotten home from my Little League game ions shuttle through consciousness producing thoughts feelings and dreams and the result is constant anxiety reason is a field marshal giving heroic directions on a battlefield choked with smoke and cannon-fire there is a need of the flesh which speaks out and tries to make itself moral transform from animal into angel Dad never read my books Mom just skimmed them I can't do without the whole notion of immortality in some form I have to accept that a million different signs prove that I will be voided eternal amnesia the last moments must be an incredible I don't believe in my own goodness I won't acknowledge it but its tears roll down my cheeks I think the worst part is knowing that you'd have been loyal to me if I'd been loyal to you I can't believe my Dad went

to work every day at six in the morning
without complaining all I did when I first
started working was pity myself one day
someone's gonna come and show us why we
were alive I chopped up my emotions into
smaller workable pieces but I can't put them
together again

stoned you to death within me I write books
that no one will read it's not as though I
wanted to write them

before she left for Europe I would go over
to my sister's apartment with N every
Sunday we'd drink Fernet or Genepy until
we were all too tired to move and then I
would have to teach in the morning so N
and I would walk home sometimes I text but
you never respond there was a moral order
beyond what I had known the fields around
your dormitory enveloped in the last sun it
stormed on the way home I thought I'd get
into an accident

grief stresses the architecture of language
the sentence is forsaken I feel like a garden
hose that someone has forgotten to shut off
the Celan book is a turbine not a novel the

northwest wind has blown Turner's ships
out to sea in deep disbelief I project myself
into infinite space all that comes into being
must be ready for a sorrowful end we're
forced to look into the terrors of existence
you can't make things other than the way
they were why does it matter if people stop
loving N and I experiment with group sex
are you still attracted to me without a third
person involved she asked yesterday

avert my eyes from looking within float out
the window into the tentative and emerging
sunlight

drowned in the grief of the heart wild sea
fires dendrites branching like quicksilver
an inquisition-like self-monitoring makes
freedom of thought next to impossible what
really matters in conversation is the electric
charge behind words at one of those hidden
frontiers almost invisible and impassable
it begins before the beginning therefore
everything is summoned from intonation
I always surrender myself to language so
brief so fragmentary

have a small paper-cut on my forefinger

have to shit where's the bathroom unbuckle
my pants pull them shit again wipe flush
with my shoe open the stall wash my hands
for at least thirty seconds with hot water
wipe them on my pants

self-awareness builds up like a toxin in the
bloodstream

dry mouth dehydrated

ask repeatedly for the reasons why
knowledge is shrouded in illusion or masked
by the mechanisms of memory consigned
to the fifth circle along with the wrathful a
word says much less than it hopes for the
ultimate foci of experience is inconsolability
my house here is painted butter yellow and
has green shutters an endless spiral of how
did this happen

unravel the processes of interpretation walk
down one flight of stairs

standing stonestill while the crowds
flow around me through the brightspace
couples kissing talking photos chatting in
the adjacent cafe sign systems need to be
interrogated broken down understood or

burned up like old railway cars blocking up the tracks I confront myself verbally as if to arrest my mind make it take account of itself and its truly terrible shortcomings mere habit synaptic wirings burst like fireworks over a river

rejected thoughts like a swarm of summer gnats devastated ocean of consciousness like Shelley I'll drown

follow the spiraling feedback loop of sex for the wrong reasons only recently have I begun to question the principle that it means something I've already forgotten your face

cruelty without forgiveness approach orgasm just to get it over with like modernist jazz wrestling with the tempo of convulsion

try to be honest with myself about these things but from start to finish I live my life like a rat in an experiment looking for a lever to pull or a chess player playing himself for amusement twice a week I go to Metrograph to watch movies I sit in the back row or the front wherever I feel most anonymous

adapt or disintegrate either way you die
everything is sucked into the zeropoint of
the end of time but until then there's the
hope that yes you might achieve something
reach for my phone let it ring

no answer someone's on the other end
watching the screen to see if it changes
Michelangelo perceives every flash of
thought that passes through the spirit frail
hollow contemptible made of glass there
is a singularity in us which no one would
or even should understand an inborn
design invisible until it emerges in the
transparency of the picture itself how does
the brain of flesh bind to the sense of the
world it's fascinating that the mind can have
imagery at all

born blue choked for oxygen chunks of
time-past melt like freezepops in a heatwave
make timepaste

old village in the mountains chewed by
goats and sheep with tinkling bells where
Pop-Pop was born there's got to be a rhythm

to the unit of thought inside the nerves of
the brain

cut everything way leave the bare voice
onstage disembodied

the wisteria is low enough that I can climb
three feet high I feel further up like I'm
climbing towards the sky scrambling
through the fallen Sycamore leaves flopping
down in the grass

half-prayer half-ditty I try to sing my
thoughts and capture them quivering like
jelly in the skull playful metaphors carry on
the literal struggle for expressive satisfaction

shivering outside her place at four in the
morning tried to kiss her she was drunk too
still feel ashamed about that because I know
exactly who it would hurt the body upholds
the frail cross of love until it topples
and makes a mark in the desert I seduce
everyone it happens unconsciously at first
but then after awhile becomes deliberate

real artists cut life into flowers create a
fragrance out of the self the other night
we saw each other on the subway just for a

second

an avalanche of one's impossibility at
every fragment of a moment tears have a
hormonal function the choked off withered
love inside me

leave the atrium cross the lobby

resented myself for falling into my father's
profession I thought teaching was beneath
me worked on a novel each morning and
evening on the subway to school as a way
of consoling and differentiating myself
eventually I called him and told him I
needed to quit he talked me through it said
it was OK which took the pressure off and
let me be who I was which was someone
different

Oceania turning twice three times
pirouetting

like a shadow nearly every statue has a
disturbing undercurrent

a stream of time divides us before we're
born from the other side of the fertile plains
of collective memory Horus and Seth the

most mysterious of the gods only truthful
hands write true poems you left Tyre at
dawn along with the migratory birds

lemonseed hempseed crushed poured out
like ribbons spattered like color across an
eggshell

with a copper knife Iris cut off his hands
threw them into the water restored for him
new hands applied fragrant ointment

emotion brightwarm like rawlight suddenly

sorrow like light through a vacuum terror
silhouetted still infantile Greektongued
symbol I see your warmskinny ankles walk
across the floor the verbs to-die and to-be-
initiated are similar in Homer time appears
as fading and then returning at once the sun
illuminates the land of the dead at night I
feel like a neurotic dying in a hospital from
nothing but unrelentingly psychic pain

drink his blood cross back outside the rain
has stopped a Mycenaean girl reciprocates
your gesture places her hands on the earth
of her thighs

meet the grief of life everywhere the tangle
of beauty a Greek vowel made concrete in
devotion to sunlight like oil through the
pores of the windows getting too old to sleep
with younger women I'm already looking
for loopholes grab my crap from coat-check
run down the stairs past the hotdog guy and
yellowcabs and schoolchildren on their way
home

through the Mariner's Gate at 85th into the
park

interpose a very deep structure between
myself and the world differentiate it into its
subcomponents break myself down

into smaller and smaller hidden pieces we're
vehicles for adaptable traits our thoughts
about ourselves are truly incidental the
human organism will spread slowly across
the cosmos like a virus

there is nothing but the stream to be
conscious of

fourteen again walking home from school
everything's so green I can't wait to put
on dry clothes and curl up under the

covers introspection serves absolutely no evolutionary purpose it's an accident don't care if my shoes get muddy I want to listen to the rain drip from the trees a constant flow of inputs multivalent swarming omnipotent hyacinth narcissus white as bone it's horrible to forget a childhood like you would a movie quit playing baseball in the middle of tryouts Dad was so disappointed it took about a decade to get over that at his last birthday we all went out to dinner I thanked him for being a good father and I meant it spread the oak leaves of childhood across his chest like medicine long spears of grass pushing through his teeth

in the first canto of the final canticle

the Fibonacci sequence occurs throughout the natural world in the genealogy of bees in the branching of trees and flowers in petal numbers pine cones pineapples and sunflowers

rebuild the church of the dead sun and rain plural like two lovers legs touching twining together like vowels in music edging south falling asleep next to you in the piercing

April twilight like a photo negative I keep
seeing it your body thin as a knife's edge
your little breasts a black thong bunched
between your buttocks spit in your mouth
slap you across the face

a serpent lies beneath the snow breathing in
a crevice of the earth waiting for the spring
snowdrops emerge from the cold ground the
skin receives moisture keeps out bacteria
the organism tightens up like a fortress in a
state of war explore my own experience like
a grave site each buried thought exhumes
itself the Lenten roses are already fading I
was afraid that my parents would die from a
very young age

keep picturing my Dad's eyes closed
like storm doors ask for release and
understanding ask for the return of lost
time return to sender the smoke around
the campfire at Lake Tupeek Pop-Pop in
his grey windbreaker talks to me in his
cigarette-stained voice myths evolve from
common roots like tigers and snow leopards
horses and mules when I first moved to New
York I'd wait for my roommates to leave

in the morning because they had jobs and I didn't and I'd drink tea and write poems on my typewriter eat avocados with a spoon read at bookstores until they closed I never paid for anything I think now that I buy books for the quick consumerist pleasure of knowing I can afford them things don't get better they get worse the earth was healthier when people died from diseases and child mortality was high I shouldn't have survived actually nature wanted to kill me off I'm wasting resources my grandmother sent a pulse of emotional trauma through our family the pulse that's still traveling through my sister

small places of presence close them up like wounds very tiny red maple blossoms head west across the park always searching for faces wrap around the southern curve of the reservoir tourists selfie by the water talent is something other than the skill of the hand that writes the trees and water and sky in the grass blue violets are poking up just like at home in the spring before anything else I would always get so angry when Dad would make me mow the lawn and kill them

Mom would wake me up singing don't know what she does in the evenings I call her sometimes it's not that I don't go home it's just too painful

walking through the pine grove push my hand into the earth spread its sweetness against the sky don't think about what my soul is feeling just register it and simultaneously push it down thoughts become compost dinosaur bones rotting at the bottom of the geosphere from the witness box I meet my own speechless gaze especially at night I accuse myself of not working hard enough of not caring enough of taking shortcuts not paying attention to what matters in a few weeks it will be warm the fields will teem with people having fun hanging out tossing a frisbee or football I've always been selfish manipulate people into adoring me tongue twisting like a kite in the wind

bound by a powerful erotic tie to my own memories in the back of my mind there is a hazy field of infinite regress human sexuality is innately perverse I open every

door but won't go in I just look undisguised
sexual curiosity about the mother sleeping
besides her at night linked and loving
wind brushes back the dusky grass a myth
mediates a discontinuity winter death
paradise lost temps perdu a series of bridges
over gulfs the melody is coming back to me
early flowers ask for nothing they sleep at
night lusty dreams usually when I've been
alone for a few nights I lost my virginity the
summer before college it was embarrassing
in my car I had no use for her afterwards
resumed my hollow existence sensual life is
just too deeply private sometimes

deviate south along a toepath a black lab
lopes after a tennis ball tropes spring up
like mushrooms under the forest floor a
network of associations stretching for miles
I've been dead in the future forever in a
semi-lethargic way I just want food maybe
another cup of coffee I can't really tell what
I want just keep walking

a caesura intervenes a silence I

see myself as if from above a figure of
absurdity self-martyred a little island

amidst chaos a jellyfish in a vast ocean of
uncertainties speckled by a few islands of
calibrated and stabilized forms this cherry
tree Pop-Pop's chicken coop cigarette smoke
in the kitchen the smell of grilled cheese
the taste of Coca-Cola I think about having
a daughter or son discarded fragments no
bridge leads us back into the heart of the
world there are so many cycles of loss of
worldliness and loss of interaction with the
outside followed by cycles of renewal don't
let me get away with acting hopeless there's
a strength that floods me a force or current
of energy I use to modulate the discovery of
this figural immensity this hidden life the
white mouth opens the serpent who takes
possession of the springs only allows the
water to flow on the condition of a human
sacrifice cherry flowers dying planets
planted like seeds

sloping southwest through the softball fields
my sister worries about how thin I've gotten
do pushups before bed put raw eggs in my
smoothie for protein I used to tell Dad to
stop eating sugar he was in good shape some
things are just bad luck the core damns up

the blood bursts through the vein-walls the organism shudders and stops like galaxies at the end of time when the stars burn out one by one like a city at night during wartime I've been poisoning my own life since I was a teenager a defense against caring too much as a child I was afraid of being seen naked or heard singing at the piano to share the stories I wrote or to even share what I was reading so great is the uncanniness of this a vision of order here comes the baseball in an arc from home plate I resented playing the outfield I wanted to be pitching it makes you hungry for achievement being overlooked when you're young at Christmas every year my cousins just get older and older have more and more kids am I the only one who isn't changing probably the love I feel for people is never strong enough to change anything about them how do you know the moon is moving look at the tides

feel calmer now

the evening comes the flood subsides birds arrive to eat the worms their graves looked old already and the shape of memory is drawn

down to the deepest level of voice

create fissure in time pass a tremor through
the hand of the future to its heart drank tea
and wrote songs that was my favorite time
of year in Syracuse I felt very stable I read
books and rode my bike I wasn't taking
many classes my last year just one or two
and just like with my high school friends I
don't really talk to anyone from that period
of my life either while writing a book I start
to worry about dying before it's done I think
it violates my need for control I'm afraid of
Citibikes use herbs I don't drink tapwater
for fear of carcinogens going to the doctor
is out of the question my eyes hurt all the
time from using my computer too much

the world is only a mirror returning to its
images

passing by the Delacorte clusters of sweet-
smelling crabapples I'm like my mother
skillfully sometimes even ethically arranging
social reality so that one's own lack of
personality is hidden the sun's almost warm

and luminous just sick of myself I waste
whole days caught up with my own internal
monologue like a spider tangled in its web
bats are among the very few wildlife that
can really adapt to human encroachment
they may have roosts in high-rises or in
trees or in crevices in the park a park like
this is heaven for diurnal bats we are visual
but they are nocturnal and acoustic we don't
cross paths very easily but they're there

a few dozen expressions permuted with
deliberate redundancy accumulate meaning
even as they emptied of it

I sucked the giddiness from your flesh
begged you to let me stop a poem should
be like reaching out and touching someone's
face enter the heart from the outside like
opening the screen door to an old house in
the country on a summer night thick with
gnats and stars

cedar trees bleached like whale bones on
the beach after a hurricane a few summers
ago when I drove down south by myself
at the end of August just to think things
over my capacity for lying to others

seems inexhaustible Shakespeare's herbs mint marigold wild thyme what else fluid intelligence thickens emulsifies slows down the process has already started the world has been stripped of thinkers like a field by locusts still can't read a book for longer than a few minutes disembodied sourceless a confused feedback loop that can't pick a signal out of its own noise

slice away the cortex and enter a state of timelessness

the quantum level exists side by side with the world as we see it every day grass and rivers bridges and buildings dogs and cats birds and sky the two domains are sides of the same coin when a mode of existence disappears there's no one to remember it no one to measure the present against the past cancer is a protest not a disease nature builds in self-destruction I think about my Dad running through clouds of DDT as a boy or inhaling secondhand smoke from his father or plastics of all kinds microwaves hairspray God knows what else he was a child of the nuclear age when science was synonymous

with progress wonder if I washed my hands
well enough

trace the transverse along 79th southwest
found so many ways of letting my friends
know that I thought that I was better than
them growing up but the trick was never to
say it but now years later they're punishing
me and I don't really blame them I didn't
want to be included

trees stooping prone like old women

birds twined with the chant of a soul
fragrant pines the cedars dusk and dim lay
the willow branches down at the threshold
of moral life Lincoln was shot 151 years ago
today all across the country his funeral train
brought mourners the banks of the rivers
grass trees stars moon the plowed-under-
earth of this island between river and ocean
in a billion years all this will be eradicated
by an expanding sun from the perspective
of satelite our lives pass in the course of a
few weeks from a distant star in the span of
less than a second living in constant panic
encoded in my cells a cascade of associations
the doctor waited too long to open her up

I was born blue bending south again along the wooded bridal path

fragmented analogy is the technique which gives rise to instantaneous effect like a bolt of lightning I've neglected my own subconscious long enough that it wants to punish me saw you on the subway platform last week with someone else saw the look on your face

animals and plants and spoken languages die everyday in droves two dogwoods situated in the backyard separated by the driveway one pink the other white clothes on the clothesline hovering over a copse of flowers along the fence like ghosts the women in my family are manic the men depressive the ecology of mind is not just the relation between open spaces or rural nature and mental space but a necessary symbiosis with the imagination we can't sustain the present world population without advanced kinds of machinery

the unhappy part of myself is betraying the poignant part I understand why N is angry given what I did two years ago it was late

and I was drunk and I exhausted but still
it was her sister with the windows open
and the snow and the cold air coming in
furtive moments of innovative closeness
fingers unbuttoning a blouse fall over catch
the curtain laughing the sun knocked over
the dried flowers on the nightstand had to
replant them dusk falls in pauses

saved from the wound of such discontinuity
by memories returning suspended in a
stream like spawning fish struggling to surge
past a dam one day my eyes will close for the
last time I'll lose contact with the earth like
a space probe that dies somewhere past the
outer rings of Jupiter the gravitational field
extends in every dimension from a random
fluctuation the universe was born in every
direction does it stop does it have a fence
like a brain has a skull does it look through
someone's eyes in the grass twilight falls
like a stone I smell the witch hazel on my
face physical tears have so much emotion
inside them like a firing squad in paralysis
unable to kill the prisoner before them

a mother of two pushes the younger in a

stroller while the elder tags along they're speaking French the boy's happy and oblivious to the world they're going to feed the duckies before it gets dark the child is conflicted between love and hate towards his parents and through internalizations turns some of his aggression on himself as a way of controlling it irony is a means of facilitating the war in the psyche they grow inaudible quickly like I'm drunk and the world is spinning what did God do before creation what was he waiting for I have arrived at my most fragile point I want to ask you things you won't tell it's interesting how people hide behind the horizon of infinity perfectly content to run out the clock out on their lives so that they don't have to acknowledge that I am waving goodbye to you all make me tame strip the nimbleness from my animal feet lay down for a second or an hour in the grass who cares about the mud fall asleep like in a movie wake up when your life's over and the credits are rolling the eye and the soul are each one half of the same idea like a knot that cannot tie itself back together on the northwest side of the lake

now imagining my inevitable destruction
and re-absorption into the cosmic whole
Prajapati the total arsenal of entropy cannot
destroy the little flashes of eternity that
a mind sees within itself set the earth's
table cup the cherry flowers in my hands
a cluster of marks on your breast spirit of
silence bitter leaves the park has the richest
subsoil in the city the cumulative meaning
of a life doesn't suffer so much from words
but elision and omission based on the pain
of being alive the unconscious is structured
like a language a network of circumstances
and glances I want everyone be captivated
by my power the city is a nervous system
radiating outwards from the spiral of my
brain

light tips over the horizon like honey from
a jar what time is it sit up getting cold have
to take a scarf from the tangle of books
notebooks pens the water-jug a half-eaten
block of cheese in my knapsack blood
pumps through the brain like hot water in
an old apartment steam hisses candle flames
in the windows under the covers happy
little boy now the sun is setting an artist

does not confess they create engulfed in the
vast spring darkness middle-aged people on
bikes get exercise I left in the middle of the
wedding to drive up to see you what do I
do when nothing is beautiful anymore the
whole method of integrating the self begins
to crumble I begin to feel like a rat in a
vast experiment ruled by impulses habits
bursts of serotonin I haven't gone a waking
hour without looking at my phone for years
because I'm trapped in the logic of the
world I live in

spring is buried a year in advance of the
winter it's all part of a deep ritual of
dreaming and waking and dying and giving
birth the relentless cycle of time concealed
in the shape of an arrow comes back to its
target the Search is for signs or systems to
organize into dominions of meaning which
in turn bestow Presence

why did Mom stop going to therapy and
start relying on her son

natal petals flower of three suns closing
under bright crowns of trees the west side
hums quietly death is as deep as the sea an

abscess that just pours out and drains away
I feel like a spy or a foreigner in some way
like I don't belong here a ghost I could
slip between the walls enter any building
without a key

when you saw the night rise in my eyes you
said

all this and then surrender

early blooming clusters of tiny snow-white
flowers on the trees which line the street
perhaps there are multiple universes and
the mind just aggregates them the way a
piano aggregates tones so when you play
a chord there are other resonances I could
have gotten hit by a car right there crossing
the street I've always lived for the few
minutes in the afternoon when the sun from
whatever angle cuts across the room and
there's polyphonic Bach on the stereo and
my thoughts are clear as a kid I liked to stay
up and listen to the adults talk over coffee at
parties I never felt like I belonged with the
other children down into the tunnel at 72nd
street and wait for the C

one day I'll relinquish my own deceptive way of relating to other people the way I never tell them the whole truth never allow insight into my own emotional state adult social gatherings involve nervous jokes TV references complaints about work bragging about accomplishments I'm always a little ashamed to be out for drinks just spending money thoughts cycle like a washing machine whirring through presets feelings actually grow stronger in response to repression they become virulent and impossible to control they want to break out

look at the veins in my wrists strong from doing pull-ups in the schoolyard down the street

underground again exhausted my socks still feel wet I'm hungry there's still some cheese in my bag maybe I should go to Whole Foods some burly guy with dyed blonde hair stares at me his mouth open a little people have no shame

haven't eliminated the possibility of catastrophic risk from the highly interconnected world-system we're building

the C train stalls at 14th I start to get fidgety
it's some kind of reflex like when a crocodile
senses movement and snaps its jaws or an
ostrich buries its head in the sand

damp skin want to take a bath after the
dog died the house was so quiet Dad
barely looked up from his computer for
weeks he looked unwell we didn't know yet
that the cancer had come back the garden
bloomed Mom clipped deadheads from the
coneflowers I knew something was wrong

get off at West 4th walk

two blocks to Caffe Reggio the equivalent
of the first frame of a film the moment
the shape of an object the color of a story
that represents an opening or a detour
a redirection whispered speech clinking
glasses and pewter cups doors opening and
closing cool air rushing in and out take off
my coat my scarf take out my notebook
my pen look around pretty crowded but
no one I know order an omelet with goat's
cheese and mushrooms and a large carrot
juice take out my notebook this novel
will not be written I will simply not write

books anymore or letters or make any other arrangements with hope it's a calamity the spell I'm casting

never liked the ashes on my forehead as a kid never knew such faith or innocence again there's no single point at which I start to make sense splintering like mercury interiority disincarnate in speech

autotelic asyntactic rendered without the beautiful logic that redeems it from bitterness this is all that's left providence stripped off like bark from a tree

check my phone no notifications no nothing crumble into impulses as if my whole body was an engine for the raising of a simple single lever or the pressing of a single button follow the fleeting glance you going one way me going the other drifting over the pages I can barely read without my glasses finally the omelet arrives show me butchers with blood on their aprons so we can see the death that comes with feeding oneself to whom is this vow addressed feeling at moments of deathlike existence all human beings are worthy of love awakening you

feel the bitterness of the unabsolved guilt
a poem is imperfect penance a hymn which
explores both the past and future a toneblot
tell me what do you see a braid of discourse
that sets you in the other's world I miss you
I don't know what I'm doing here I text you
all the time to get a drink no response of
course rapid aerial view of the shapeless
depths I keep expecting a text from my Dad
loss grows roots like vines in a desert this
place is cash only I have just enough for a
tip don't want to make a bad impression
the regulars are smoking outside we never
speak to each other the literati love the life
of an inconceivable emptiness reading each
other's Tweets I always have this suspicion
that it's everyone else who is experiencing
the world in a real way and that I'm just
faking it copying their behavior creating the
complex illusion that I'm feeling anything
at all

spill out onto 6th Avenue like floodwater

light-torrent

wept and twisted around my fingers last
night we talked about everything about how

intense we both are and how emotional her
mouth closed over mine

open and hermetic flesh and bread

dead black sky paper mache self-
deconstructing heart poke holes in the
tissue energy pours through my art runs
through itself like a fugue a self-generating
universe neurons die like stars in the brain
on a deeper level there is an understanding
which forbids itself forgiveness

a place where language gathers around that
core from which it gains truth

my father's father died in the middle of the
night in the morning Dad had tears in his
eyes that's all I remember

electric signs orbit around gleams of
abstraction coffee flowers organic products
diary lotto cigarette beer soda EBT ATM
we buy electronics we fix phones jewelry
express shoe and watch repair

entropy creates what we perceive as time
lost summers the dog sunning at my feet
Dad mowing the lawn Mom digging in the

garden Eda upstairs sewing

immerse myself in contemplation of the
sidewalk my mood is free for a moment
of all desire existence slips like gold coins
through my fingers close the loop around
my neck hang me from the beams of reality

nothing reveals the world better than our
presence in it I feel this pressure to be on all
the time I can't forgive the dead for dying
would join them if I could time is marked in
subtle ways left without saying goodbye this
morning my Metrocard is almost empty

survey myself as I would a dead planet
in the future strewn with relics of a lost
civilization

make the desert cry out cold dark city like
a broken heart experience splits meaning
open joggers cyclists strangers along the
river

language speaks only itself before the brain
breaks it into pieces on the tongue

a harmonic and contrapuntal structure
rather than beautiful notes

your question your answer your song

kneeling at the river Mnemosyne which runs dark with blood or on the east bank of the Nile unable to cross fishing fragments from the river all the firstborn of Egypt lay dead

Mom chops vegetables for dinner N keeps talking about the child we gave up

drown

harmonically and instrumentally I touch your fingers floating like a shroud

drove out to the beach with my friends in the middle of winter ten years ago I went down to the beach in the biting wind and tore myself apart

if there is no beginning to find then you have to search until the end of eternity the pressure's unbearable children sleep flowers sprout from their eyelids the wheel of time rolls out of itself the spokes disappear only stones survive this prodigy of gloaming the skyline is a hovering Eucharist he shines in the sky two dreams falling like morning and evening stars innocent Abel in Cain's body self-smiting in the nothingness of night

a multiple a composite

the birdcatchers have gone silent the washerwomen have gone back home drunk on lotus petals

instructions lamentations dialogues

secure against loss glowing like a sun deep in a far off galaxy its light just now arriving my fingers are cold the temperature's dropped it's snowing I'm brushing my teeth there's no school tomorrow three feet are supposed to fall Eda and I will make an igloo Dad will plow the sidewalks with the neighbor's snow blower

at the river cradle where the sea becomes a second heart

hail a cab want to go anywhere it doesn't matter maybe home

sorrow and feeling pass into the foreign tongue I invent so as to remain blameless if nobody reads it

an unbroken chain of dawns rattles in the
skull another one's coming at Plank-scale
where space shatters and foams

eyes like poisonous weeds torn out

motionless inside the photograph your lips
are cold against my teeth

crossing the bridge the old moon left
hanging

nightstump

wasted pearl today in reverse

made coffee filled a bowl with roses I don't
know how to cope with the loss of light

the cab driver tells me about his childhood in
Pakistan he was a farmer they raised cotton
and rice had cows and buffalos and sheep he
wants to go back one day when his children
are older missing contact with babies and
animals herbs and microorganisms nutrients
and dirt in general

an amputated self grows back like a tentacle

buried recollection involuntary memory a doubling effect that amplifies the amplitude of time you were there on my bed the heat wasn't working we drank wine in the living room your mom called you talked on the phone

in a small black notebook under Russian occupation to earn money Celan did translations meanwhile another cold winter set in there were food shortages I'm building a turbine not a novel I can only cycle back to the beginning buried in the poetry of the earth without context or comprehension

the levels are linked discretely my attention picks up I see the heart through the brain we had friends over they looked through our records our books drank I was bored N didn't want a threesome she wanted to sleep with Z alone but how was I supposed to know she's jealous of the women I see on the side because I'm not jealous of the women she sees on the side analytic thought is a knife to cut these voices down to one

his last hours

dead deity dangling from a dazzled sun undreamed of dark black broken bread four circles three crosses

never leave the depths and keep holding dialogue with the wellspring winding through Brooklyn like a snake over the water the streets are empty except for cop cars and delivery men on bicycles and ubers loitering in the bus lanes you woke up first put on Molly Drake on Spotify the sun was pouring in like lust I looked at you sorrowing god swam to the bottom and held my breath as a teenager I saw lights behind my eyes I wasn't getting enough oxygen for years

our personality is what flows through time the self endures a continuous flux or succession of states an unfolding coil or a continually rolling ball of thread

pay the driver

what will Mom do now will she go on dates start over at this age

experiencing it all over again listening to the rain after school it all goes dark now many generations past my ancestors toiling in the fields receiving micronutrients from the leaves and flowers they came into contact with I wasn't born from my mother's womb so I wasn't coated with the fluid of the birth canal which produced the first of many millions of degrees of separation from the world of beasts

slowly open the door

like a marathon runner reporting the news of the victory back to Athens I arrive halfdead running on the fumes of nonexistence kiss her neck my phone was off are you upset no but she's lying I have to pee so I roll off the couch

leafing fingers where were you I guess it doesn't matter

curling up on the couch spoon her stroke her hair

M we're not alright

haven't been alright for awhile

surface once like the moon from behind the

clouds hands push through the covers and
flap like faded or mangled wings the two
sides of us were asked to suffer when pulled
apart like decimated echoes nothing created
by God is subject to destruction Beatrice
says let's go to sleep

my eyes reach for the oxygen in my lungs
my hands refuse to explode with everything
left unsaid inside play the tape forward just
yesterday we were listening to Nina Simone
in the living room and we were laughing
look at her

drowned in lovedeath and then somehow
released back up again

a gradual syntactical unfolding

the unmistakable voice of spiritual ekstasis
the last part an invitation to carnality

rivet my kisses to her ribs and neck

the body is broken up like a river choked
by ice

a highly nuanced aesthetic form capable of
bearing the immense weight of the

feel the light which radiates from the still
open eye spiritual life just means a way out
of the morass it doesn't matter where to
heaven or nirvana or the ashtray it just has
to be different love does not distinguish cry
from cry heart from heart I never knew the
earth dark and damp as if with our blood
there is shape and symmetry I light the
fire with your hair I woke up dreaming the
meek shall be exalted bring out the dead
Jacob saw climbing from their graves put
my body in a canoe with flowers and fire
send trails of wine down the river after me
Mom fell from the radiator when she was
pregnant with my sister trying to hang
curtains Eda was almost miscarried the
future dilates each harvest brings pleasure
to the house and heavy labor for you Osiris
slice your bread with a pocket knife eat the
crumbs from the floor

fracture the music along the lines of melody
hear each part again like it was your singing
voice it will go on for ages like this like a
shadow blindly chasing itself around the

house

with deliberate redundancy a permutation-
poem choked off a withered love inside me
wrest a last work of ferocious beauty from
the depths of futility and despair

can't have my children sweet bloom of
the-far-away knees curled up to her chin
hair fallen over her face like a little boy's
gutted smeared with gold pick up our bones
throw up earthworks I'm here that's all that
matters slip my hand under the fabric of her
underwear carry her to the bedroom I was
born blue just talk to me I don't know why
I avoid confrontation kiss the stubbly blond
hairs on her legs her pubis her ass her slender
back lean arms small breasts black hairs
poke up around the nipples which I pluck
with my teeth she howls in pain and maybe
even pleasure light a candle make more tea
wake back up Ornette Coleman very loud I
said be grateful be still before this was real
it was true the earth reels to and fro like
a drunkard you were my dreamlife we had
dreamchildren lulling me out of deliberate
dissociation in the slanted lamplight you

can go back to your life but I have to keep
living in this one the heart's home is early-
chosen late-lamented on the brink of deep
night we encircle the sun clouds pile up the
moon begins its long labor of giving birth
to the ocean of mourning the magic ship
arrives bearing the gifts of flame and iron
self-governing Svāhā blessing try to sleep
while long blue meteors chase the weariness
away I'm in the grave already resurrect
me kiss my neck just like that baths are a
bid for health taken up when she's tired
or nervous working a restorative cure for
the claustrophobic tensions of our little
apartment hot water purifies and muddies
at once time consuming and dehydrating
the rest of the apartment is dark I'm waiting
in the living room half-asleep an arch-
opportunist cut ties with the past float like
a balloon into the upper atmosphere burst
and fall in fragments like a Roman candle
tonight is perfectly clear tomorrow will
be warmer the greenstuff will insist on its
on growth after a million years it may be
impossible for creatures for another planet
to detect that human beings were ever here
jumping from metonymy to metonymy it's

all cold outside gooseflesh and the sound
of her breathing tender Egyptian statuette
tomorrow the curtain will catch the sunlight
the day will be clear I'll unfreeze some
bonebroth add tumeric and butter have
a savory breakfast good for the tendons
and teeth the deepest part of the mind is
perfect and knows itself if I don't write this
book now like really write it I never will
and maybe that's what needs to happen
acceptance or acknowledgement of what's
been broken and can't get put back together
when the semantic and logical associations
that bind us together disintegrate so do we
words knows their origins and acts as an
intermediary with the context you endow
through speaking the primitive places the
forests the old oaks the cut-down places a
way out of the mesh of habits we call sexual
freedom the violent reaction against the
fertility of the body I've killed so much
unwanted life sperm ova embryos weeds
insects I can't masturbate because I'll start
to think about you the good part of existing
is not being separate from others I feel
guilty about porn I used to watch it but now
it just makes me depressed I'm too tired for

sex most of the time I've been drawn and quartered scattered to the four winds cancer is the natural outcome of poisoned fields microwaves and plastics and pesticides the earth is planted in space like a vegetable its roots nourished by the sun we've cut the ties between eating and farming loving and creating life and what does this mean the good divided among the bad like jacks in a deck of cards in the old garden this spring never have I seen so many butterflies in the worm-state a little central cylinder the only flesh is the worm an avalanche of one's impossibility at every fragment of a moment the animal with the first nervous system might have been the jellyfish something with no shell or skeleton probably hovering in the water a filmy lightbulb despite all my theories there's a wordgap a vacancy the politics of emotion are indistinguishable from neurosis a divided self argues about procedures and the spirit of the laws empty speech after the fall without Adam's power of naming a comedown from God-given speech halting doubled-back dividing and divided a translation two angels arrived at Sodom by evening ashes driven through

the furrowing wind half-finished forever
Celan was not a German he just wrote in
the master's language it was a form of self-
torture ritual abasement and purification
that's what attracts me to the subject sacred
time is discontinuous I'm a skull a dreamer
asleep in a cave break down my defenses
boundaries blindspots borders my sister will
have children one day seal off the eruptive
shocks my mother's wrinkles carnal century
cyclical longing death and revival for the act
of resignation faith is required a memory of
a future which will not arrive the universe
is like the seed in the fruit transforming
the nutrients of empty space into a tree I'm
obsessed with Haydn's prism-like forms as
complex as anything human beings have
created an artist is a spy from an invisible
country you're just beginning cut a slit
pull out the innards and inwardness white
violents the bed frame's glowing with
radium reach for a Melatonin time to shut
off close the screen disappear like being dead
but I don't want to die I want to live affirm
this like a bird fluttering upward life is one
long night Oedipus says to Tiresias the city
for which I'm writing this for will perish in

the brain of my childhood room the window is open here's a warm body gently kiss her knees wretched little monster I held the soul of my child in my teeth the great egg of America fertilized by my peasant ancestors I can hear the garbage trucks outside pull the petals off the days uncomb your hair lick my eyelids a contrapuntal exercise her last mood is always Mahler put on the 4th we won't sleep tonight or maybe we will peel off the night with protective gloves watch the birds in the blue daybreak transfiguration is a voluntary act a seal printed on the dead marks them for return as the ships set sail and like the hidden bird that sang even if Time is abolished we will still exist in the twisted syntax of your speech seeking sight and like a downpour you painted the world with your presence and in the fragments of a dead language I named you Lost Love and it's raining today because that's what the spring is for and because it's the beginning of a book